GW01066232

Rex Plays

Story by Julie Haydon
Illustrations by Pat Reynolds

Every afternoon, Jacob and Mum
walked over to the park
with their dog, Rex.
Jacob always put a tennis ball
in his pocket.

When they reached the park,
Jacob pulled out the ball
and slowly lifted his arm.
Rex barked with excitement.
He ran round and round in circles.
Rex loved playing fetch.

One day, Jacob threw the ball
as far as he could.
"Fetch!" he shouted.

Rex raced after the ball.
He ran so fast
that he had to skid to a stop!

Rex grabbed the ball in his mouth
and rushed back with it.
He dropped the ball at Jacob's feet
and waited for him
to throw it again.

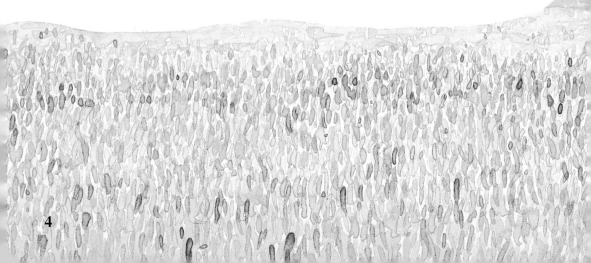

4

This time, Rex jumped into the air
and caught the ball
before it hit the ground.

"You play fetch better
than any other dog I know,"
said Jacob proudly.

Jacob threw the ball again.
This time it went near some bushes.

Rex raced after the ball
and skidded into the bushes.
Then he gave a loud yelp
and backed out,
holding one paw in the air.
It was bleeding.
Rex had cut it on some glass.

Jacob and Mum rushed over to Rex.

"That's a bad cut," said Mum.
"We need to take him to the vet."

The vet looked at Rex's paw.
"This cut is quite deep," he said.
"It needs to be stitched.
I'll have to put him to sleep for a while,
so I can do it."

The vet stitched Rex's paw
and put a bandage on it.

Later, Jacob and Mum
came to pick up Rex.

Rex didn't like the bandage.
He tried to lick it off.

"How can we stop him
from doing that?" asked Jacob.

The vet gave them a plastic collar
that looked like a cone.
"He will have to wear this
for a few days," said the vet.

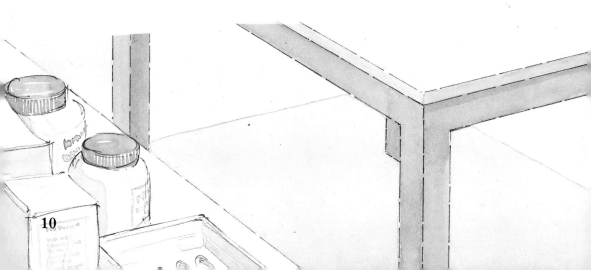

Rex didn't like the collar,
or the bandage, at all.
His paw hurt if he tried to walk on it.
He limped around the backyard.
He couldn't run.

"Do you think Rex will ever
be able to play fetch again?"
Jacob asked his mother.

"I hope so," said Mum,
"but we'll have to wait and see."

Ten days later,
the vet took the stitches out.
Rex's paw was much better.

When he stopped limping,
Jacob and Mum took him
for a walk in the park.

Jacob had the tennis ball
in his pocket.
He took it out
and slowly lifted his arm.

Rex barked with excitement,
and ran round in circles.

"Fetch!" shouted Jacob.
He threw the ball away from the bushes.

Rex gave a happy yip.
He sped across the grass,
grabbed the ball,
and ran back with it.

"Mum," cried Jacob.
"Rex is just as good at fetch
as he used to be!"